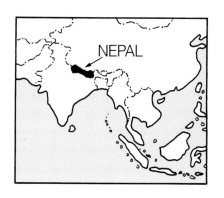

NEPAL

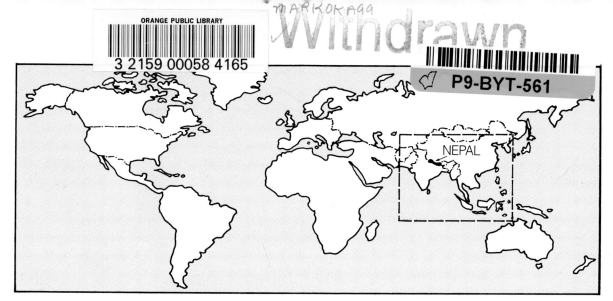

NEPAL

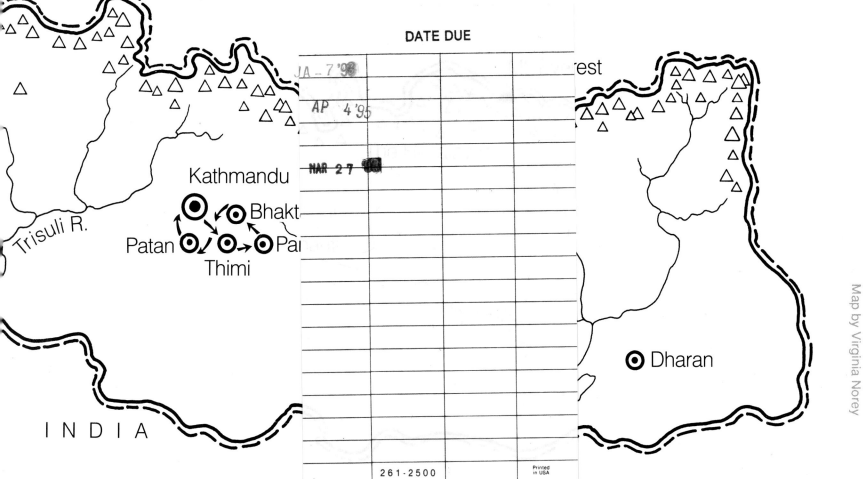

Trisuli R.

Kathmandu

Patan ○→○→○ Par

Bhakt

Thimi

⊙ Dharan

INDIA

rest

Map by Virginia Norey

Kanu of Kathmandu
A Journey in Nepal

Barbara A. Margolies

Four Winds Press ⁂ New York

Maxwell Macmillan Canada   Toronto
Maxwell Macmillan International
New York   Oxford   Singapore   Sydney

A warm thanks to His Excellency Ambassador Jayaraj Acharya for his thoughtful reading of my manuscript, his linguistic expertise, and his hospitality.
—B.A.M.

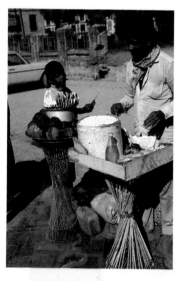

093499

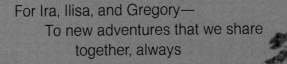

For Ira, Ilisa, and Gregory—
To new adventures that we share
together, always

Namaste, and welcome to Nepal!

For over one hundred years, visitors were rarely permitted to enter my country. In 1951 our borders were opened to the outside world. Today I invite the children of the United States to see my beautiful homeland.

Nepal is home to many different people and diverse cultures, all living together peacefully. From the green valley of Kathmandu to the snowcapped peaks of the Himalayas, enjoy this journey in Nepal.

Raamro sanga ghumnos, travel in peace.
Namaste.

जयराज आचार्य

Jayaraj Acharya
Ambassador
Permanent Representative of Nepal
to the United Nations

Surrounded by the giant countries of China and India is the tiny kingdom of Nepal. Eight-year-old Kanu Sengupta lives in Nepal's capital city, Kathmandu.

This morning Kanu has come to work with his father, Utpal Sengupta. Kanu's father is the general manager of the busy Hotel Shangri-la.

Today Kanu will go with his father's friends on a tour of several small cities and villages outside Kathmandu. Kanu is excited about the trip and eager to get going! He is looking forward to being a tour guide.

Finally they are on their way. Out on the road they see many large trucks.
"A lot of people can squeeze on board those trucks," says Kanu.

Going further away from Kathmandu city, Kanu passes farms.

"Most people in Nepal are farmers. They grow vegetables, fruit, wheat, and rice. Maybe I'll be a farmer when I grow up," says Kanu. "The seeds from all those yellow flowers will be made into mustard. My *ama*, mother, uses them when she cooks.

"See those little grass huts on top of the poles? Sometimes a farmer has to spend the night in the hut so he can chase away animals that come to eat his crops. I would be afraid to stay alone there! Hmm, maybe I won't be a farmer!

"Look! That farmer has made a really big haystack!" shouts Kanu. "It would be fun to climb to the top and slide down!"

"*Namaste,* hello," says Kanu to a man carrying pots. "Did you make those?"

"Yes, and now I'm on my way to market to sell them," answers the man.

In the village of Panauti, they park the Jeep and Kanu buys an orange.

"*Yó suntala ko kati parchha?*" asks Kanu in the Nepali language. "How much is this orange?"

"One rupee," answers the woman.

Every day this woman and her friends come down from their mountain homes to sell their fruit in the village. They are called hill people.

Everywhere people are busy working. This man, Mangal, and his father are beating sun-dried millet to separate the flower pod from the stem.

"*Namaste,*" says Mangal. "Would you like to try this?"

"Ohhh, this is hard work," says Kanu, as he pounds the millet with all his strength.

Kanu watches as Mangal's sister separates the outer husks from the seeds. She throws them up in the air over and over again. When she has enough seeds, they will be ground into flour to make bread.

As Kanu walks through the village streets, children are playing everywhere. Kanu explains why many children in Nepal don't go to school.

"A lot of families can't afford the school fees. And many villages don't even have schools! I go to the Badaboum School in Kathmandu. There are lots of European and Nepalese kids in my school. I'm in grade three, and I study English, French, Nepali, history, geography, science, and mathematics. Geometry is my favorite subject.

"If kids don't go to school," continues Kanu, "they have to help on the farm or learn a craft from their fathers—like making puppets or clay figures and pots."

"Do you want to play paddleball with us?" asks one of the boys.

"Do you want some sugarcane?" yells another boy.

"*Dhanyabad,* thank you, but I am busy being a guide today," answers Kanu.

In all of the places Kanu visits—Thimi, Panauti, Bhaktapur, and Patan—he passes old, old houses. The Nepalese people have carved beautiful designs around their windows.

Walking up and down the streets, Kanu points out the mothers spinning or winding wool and knitting caps and sweaters.

"It's cold in the early morning and at night," says Kanu. "*Ama* knits sweaters for me, too! And scarves for *Ba*, Father! Did you see that some of the ladies have red marks on their foreheads? The marks mean that they are married."

People are busy doing many different things—making bread, carrying heavy loads, selling meat or cloth, peanuts or rice.

"I wonder if I weigh as much as a bag of rice!" says Kanu, as he jumps onto a scale.

"I guess these old men don't work anymore. They like to sit and talk and smoke pipes. Their hats are called *topis*. A *topi* is the traditional Nepali cap."

As Kanu leaves the village, he stops and quietly watches a man pray over the burning funeral pyre of a relative. Kanu explains that the pyre is built on a *ghat,* an area on the bank of a river. When the fire has burned out, the ashes will be thrown into the river.

"It is part of the Hindu tradition," whispers Kanu.

He points to the snowcapped mountains in the distance. Acting just like a grown-up guide, Kanu says, "We have some really big mountains. They are called the Himalayas. And Mount Everest is the highest peak in the whole world! When I am older, *Ba* and I will climb one of them—maybe Mount Everest or Annapurna. It will be like climbing into the sky!"

In the cities of Bhaktapur and Patan, Kanu stops to see some Hindu and Buddhist temples.

"There are real gold figures and designs on a lot of the temples. I like the statues with all the hands!" says Kanu. "Many of the temples were built hundreds of years ago.

"People make *puja,* offerings, to the different gods, inside or outside the temples. They leave rice, tea, and flowers. And this man will say prayers and give offerings for you. But you have to pay him!"

Back again in Kathmandu, Kanu leads his group along the crowded streets.

"Wait!" says Kanu. "I have to get this hat. I need it for when I play soldier. *Yasko kati parchha?* How much is this?"

"Three rupees, *dhanyabad,*" answers the storekeeper.

"These puppets are nice. Maybe I'll buy one for my friend Devi. I know these ladies. *Ama* buys fish from them."

"We have so many different people in Nepal. And you can see them all in Kathmandu. Some are Sherpas, some are Gurungs, or Newars or Tamangs, Magars or Rais. I learned all about the people of Nepal in history class.

"Look! There are three Buddhist monks. Oh, there is a *sadhu*, a holy man, with a snake!" says Kanu. "Let's get away....I am afraid of snakes!"

"Now I want to show you a statue I really like," says Kanu. "It is called *Kalbhairav*. There is an old tale that says if a person tells a lie in front of *Kalbhairav*, the god will cause the person to spit blood! Then everyone knows the person is a liar. I wonder if it still happens.

"Hurry now. I want to go to the *Hanuman Dhoka,* the old royal palace. That's *Hanuman,* the monkey god. I guess he guards the palace. And there are real guards, too. They're called *Gurkhas.*"

On the way home, Kanu passes a wedding procession. In a Hindu marriage ceremony, a musical band plays outside the bride's house. Later the band leads the car carrying the bride and groom through the streets to the final wedding celebration. The bride is shy because she doesn't know her husband very well.

"Hindu marriages are arranged by the parents and sometimes the bride and groom meet for the first time at the wedding! I am going to pick my *own* wife!" says Kanu.

When Kanu arrives home, he rushes in to find his mother. The housekeeper, Bimla, tells Kanu that his mother is still working in her shop downtown and will be home later. Kanu waits impatiently for his parents to return home.

"Oh, *Ba*! Oh, *Ba*! I have so much to tell you. Thank you, *Ba*, for letting me be a guide today!"

Late into the night Kanu tells his parents about his wonderful day. "*Ba*," he says, "do you think we could really climb a mountain someday?"

"Yes, Kanu," says his father, "someday."

Here are some words from Kanu's journey you can learn to say in Nepali.

English word	Nepali word written in English alphabet	Nepali pronunciation*	Nepali word
Annapurna	annapurna	[aṅ na poor naa]	अन्नपूर्ण
Bhaktapur	bhaktapur	[bhaḱ ta poor]	भक्तपुर
Buddhist	buddhist	[buḋ dhist]	बुद्धिष्ट
China	chin	[chiṅ]	चीन
father	ba	[baá]	बा
ghat	ghat	[ghaaṫ]	घाट
good-bye	namaste	[na maś te]	नमस्ते
Gurkha	gorkhali	[goŕ khaa lee]	गोर्खाली
Gurung	gurung	[goó roong]	गुरुङ
Hanuman Dhoka	hanuman dhoka	[huṅ oo maan dhò kaa]	हनुमान ढोका
hello	namaste	[na maś te]	नमस्ते
Himalaya mountains	himalaya parbat	[hi maa la ya pur but]	हिमाल्य पर्बत
Hindu	hindu	[hiṅ doo]	हिन्दू
holy man	sadhu	[saá dhoo]	साधु
India	bharat	[bhaṅ rut]	भारत
Kalbhairav	kalbhairav	[kaal bhai rub]	काल्भैरव
Kanu	kanoo	[kaá noo]	कानू
Kathmandu	kathmandu	[kaaṫ maan doo]	काठमाण्डू

English word	Nepali word written in English alphabet	Nepali pronunciation*	Nepali word
Magar	magar	[muǵ ur]	मगर
millet	kodo	[koń doh]	कोदो
mother	ama	[aań maah]	आमा
Mount Everest	sagarmatha	[sá gar maa thaa]	सगरमाथा
Nepal	nepal	[naý paal]	नेपाल
Newar	newar	[naý waar]	नेवार
Panauti	panauti	[pa naú tee]	पनौती
Patan	patan	[paá tan]	पाटन
offering	puja	[poó jaa]	पूजा
Rai	rai	[raá ee]	राई
rupee	rupiya	[roó pi yaa]	रूपिया
Sherpa	sherpa	[sheŕ paa]	शेर्पा
Tamang	tamang	[taá maang]	तमाङ
thank you	dhanyabad	[dhań ney baad]	धन्यवाद
Thimi	thimi	[teá mee]	ठिमी
Tibet	tibbat	[tiŕ but]	तिब्बत
Topi	topi	[toń pee]	टोपी
truck	trak	[truǩ]	ट्रक

*In Nepali there is no emphasis put on any one syllable.

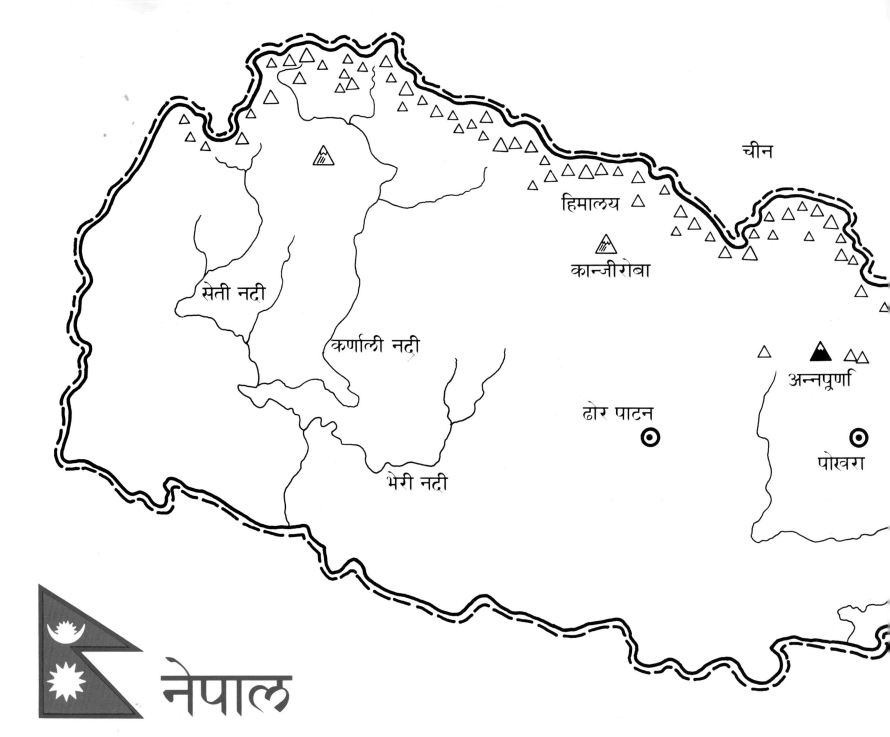

चीन

हिमाल्य △

कान्जीरोबा

सेती नदी

कर्णाली नदी

अन्नपूर्ण

ढोर पाटन ◉

भेरी नदी

पोखरा

नेपाल

The labels on this map are written in Nepali, the language of Nepal.